John D Lowes

Stenography

Shorthand Writing

John D Lowes

Stenography
Shorthand Writing

ISBN/EAN: 9783337396558

Printed in Europe, USA, Canada, Australia, Japan

Cover: Foto ©Andreas Hilbeck / pixelio.de

More available books at **www.hansebooks.com**

STENOGRAPHY,

OR

SHORTHAND WRITING;

WITHOUT A MASTER.

BY

JOHN D. LOWES,

TWENTY-TWO YEARS CHIEF REPORTER, "NEWCASTLE DAILY JOURNAL."

ENTERED AT STATIONERS' HALL.

LONDON:

WALTER SCOTT, 14 PATERNOSTER SQUARE,

AND NEWCASTLE-UPON-TYNE.

[AND ALL BOOKSELLERS.]

1883.

MY apology for adding another to the many systems of Shorthand is that the art deserves more attention than it receives, and that I have carried it farther than those from whom I received it.

I do not mean that I have discovered any principles which had not been laid down by my predecessors, from Dr. MAVOR, in the last century, to Mr. GEO. BRADLEY, in the present. MR. BRADLEY was editor of a well-known newspaper, the Newcastle *Guardian*, and not only an expert Shorthand writer, but also the author of the best system I have seen, and I have seen and examined nearly a hundred. Writing by sound is the basis of all; but, in assigning the simplest signs to the sounds most frequently occurring in the English language, I believe I have carried the principle further than anyone else.

As now published, this system is the result of test and practice begun forty years ago; and it is published in the hope that others will find Shorthand as pleasant and profitable as it has been to me.

39 WESTMORLAND ROAD, NEWCASTLE-UPON-TYNE,
3d September 1883.

ALPHABET.

a . a, an, and
b ᴄ be, been, bee, boy, by, buy, buoy, ebb
c   (*no* c : *same sound as* s, *or* k)
d ᐳ aid, add, day, do, die, due, odd
e . every
f \ of, off, if, fie, foe, for, from
g ᴏ age, ago, again, against, go, good, god
h ᴗ he, has, have, had, hay, how, high, him
i ˙ eye, I, impossible
j ᴏ joy, just, judge
k ⌒ can, could, knew, oak, ache, key
l / all, ail, ale, ill, eel, oil
m ᵪ am, aim, may, me, my, most, among, amongst
n ᴗ in, inn, on, own, know, no, nigh, not
o , oh, owe, opportunity
p ρ pay, place, point, put, up, upon
q ᶿ question
r / air, are, ire, err, her, our
s — as, ass, ease, ice, is, ooze, see, sigh, so, us, use
t | aught, at, ate, it, ought, tie, tea, to, too, toe
u / whatever
v \ eve
w ᴏᵥ awe, was, way, we, weigh, will, with, woe, would
x   (*same sound as* k, *or* ks)
y ᴠ aye, yea, ye, you, your, yours
ʒ   (*same as* s)
    / full stop

a is a point, at the line [supposed]; *b*, a half-
circle ; *c* sounds the same as *s* or *k*, and is written
accordingly ; *d*, a half-circle ; *e*, a point, below ; *f*, a
line ; *g*, a loop and line ; *h*, a hook and line ; *i*, a
point, above ; *j* is written the same as g ; *k*, a half
circle ; *l*, a line, begun from the top ; *m*, a loop and
line ; *n*, a half-circle ; *o*, a tick, below, struck downwards ; *p*, a loop and line ; *q*, a loop and line ; *r*, a
line, begun from the bottom ; *s*, a line ; *t*, a line ;
u, a tick, above, struck downwards ; *v* is written the
same as *f* ; *w*, a loop and half-circle ; *x* is written the
same as *k*, or, when strongly sounded, as in tax, *ks*.
y, a hook and line ; *z* is written the same as *s*.
full stop, a line twice the length of *l*.

DOUBLE, TREBLE, AND QUADRUPLE CONSONANTS.

bn	⌣	bean, bin, boon
bb	(	babe
ch	⌐	change, church, each, much, such
dd	)	dead, deed, died, did
kk	⌒	cake, kick, cock, cook
mm	⌐	maim
nd	)	end
nn	⌣	known, none, nun, onion, union
gn	~	
or		gain, gone, join, Jane, John, June
jn	~	
ph	＼	(same sound as *f*)
pp	ρ	pipe, pope, pup
pr	۹	par, pare, pair, pear, poor, power, pure
sh	۹	ash, show, shy, shall, should

sh   *e*   English, Englishman
shb   ℮   shabby
shd   ꙋ   shade, shod
th   /   they, thy, thou, though, them, that, this
th   ╲   without, month, something
th   ℓ   unworthy
wd   ꙅ   wade, wed, wide, wood
wh   ⌐   what, which, who, whom, why
wk   ⌒   walk, weak, week
str   ℘   star, starry, stair, stare, strange, stir, store,
           storey, strong, strength
thr   ℘   author, ether, either, other, their, there.
           thorough, through, therefore
prpr   q   prepare, proper

    bb, dd, kk, and *nn* are formed by doubling the size
of the half-circle for the single letter; *ch, pr,* and
two forms of *th,* are, in each case, a line and loop ;
gn, or *jn,* is a loop and half-circle ; *mm, pp,* and *prpr*
are formed by doubling the size of the circle of the
single letter; *nd* is a half-circle, begun at the bottom ; *sh* is a loop and half-circle ; *shb* is the *sh* combined with the *b ; shd* is the *sh* combined with the *d,*
th (first) is a hook and line ; second and third *th* is
a loop and line ; *wh* is a hook and line ; *wd* is the *w*
and the *d* combined ; *wk* is the *w* and the *k* combined : *str* and *thr* are each a loop and line ; for
prpr the size of the loop of *pr* is doubled.

    Having two characters for *sh,* and two for *th,* are
for ease of joining ; as,   ⅄   earth ;   ⅃   death ;
   ℮   ship ;   ℘   shipper.

RULES FOR WRITING.

1. Join all the letters of a word from beginning to end.
2. Except when necessary, omit all vowels in words, and all silent consonants.
3. Write according to sound, and not according to spelling.

MODES OF CONTRACTION.

There are several modes of contraction. Many words and phrases are shortened by being divided into Prefixes and Terminations, and this contraction is shown by the letters being disjoined, and placed one above the other,—as *circumstance*, written = ; and *House of Commons*, written ⌐⌐

PREFIXES.

d ꜱ de, di, distin, discon, dissatis, disinter
f ＼ fellow, for
h ⌐ hend, hension, hensive, hyper,
i ˙ incom, incompre, incon, incontro, imper, impor, impro, impru, intel, inter, intra, intro, intru
k ⌒ contra, contro, contri, compre, compri, compro, countr, counter, kingd
m ⌐ major, mercan, miscon, multi, misfor
n ⌣ in, unfor
r ／ recon
s — circum, satis, straight, super, supre
t | tran, trans
w ⌒ with
x ⌒ extra, extin
nd ꜱ under

TERMINATIONS.

d	)	dence, dent, dental, draw, drawn, drew
f	\	ficiency, firm-ed-ing-ation, form-ed-ing-ation-ality, forward
g	⌒	gent, guish
h	⌣	held, hold, hend, hensive
k	⌒	clude, clusive, country, creatures
o	⁄	ordinary
p	ρ	plant, plete
q	⁄	quil-ity-ized
s	—	scribe, scription, citizen, stance, stant-ial, stand, stinct-ion
t	/	tent, tract, tunate-ly

ARBITRARY TERMINATIONS.

ing ; thus :— . ⟋ eating, ⌿ saying, ρ paying, ∫ praying
ment ; thus :— — moment, ⟩ parliament,
cian, sion, tion ; thus :— ⌣ physician, — session, ∫ option

Other Modes of Contraction are :—

1. By omitting subordinate words, such as *of* and *the ;*

2. By placing above or below the line the initial letter of words; as, ⌒ ignorance ; ⌒ concern, and by putting letters through each other ; as, ⅌ Prime Minister; ⟋ with regard to ;

3. By writing only so much of a word as will lead to the whole ; as, ⌐ sufficient ;

4. By writing words colloquially : as, ⟨ you'll have been ; and

5. By joining pronouns and auxiliary verbs : as, ⌒⟩ we would have been

Examples of each of these modes of contraction are given; and Reporters, knowing that very much depends upon context, adopt for themselves all or any of these modes.

The examples of contractions given, according to each mode, are what I myself have been in the habit of using during the past five-and-twenty years.

Figures are one form of shorthand; and numbers are best written in them.

ARBITRARY CONTRACTIONS.

×	consider, Christian.
⸲ᛉ	Christianity.
┼	Christ.
†	Jesus Christ.
⊥	Christ Jesus.
⊹	sometimes.
┼	at the same time.
∘	one, once, ones.
○	world.
ϙ	Scripture.
⇁	Holy Ghost.
o	opponent.
℗	plaintiff.
ⱦ	defendant.
⨍	advantage.
∴	independent.
⑂	et cetera.

EXAMPLES.

THE LORD'S PRAYER.

Our Father, which art in heaven, Hallowed be

Thy Name. Thy kingdom come. Thy will be done

on earth, As it is in heaven. Give us this day our

daily bread. And forgive us our trepasses, As we

forgive them that trespass against us. And lead us

not into temptation ; But deliver us from evil ; For

Thine is the kingdom, the power, and the glory, For

ever and ever. Amen.

PSALM lxvii.

God be merciful unto us, and bless us, and shew

us the light of His countenance, and be merciful unto

us; that Thy way may be known upon earth ; Thy

saving health among all nations.   Let the people

praise Thee, O God ; yea, let all the people praise

Thee.   O let the nations rejoice and be glad ; for

Thou shalt judge the folk righteously, and govern the

nations upon earth.   Then shall the earth bring forth

her increase ; and God, even our own God, shall give

us His blessing.   God shall bless us, and all the ends

of the world shall fear Him.   Glory be to the Father,

and to the Son, and to the Holy Ghost ; as it was in

the beginning, is now, and ever shall be, world

without end.   Amen.

1 CORINTHIANS xiii. 1.

Though I speak with the tongues of men and of angels, and have not charity, I am become as sounding brass, or a tinkling cymbal. And though I have the gift of prophecy, and understand all mysteries, and all knowledge ; and though I have all faith, so that I could remove mountains, and have not charity, I am nothing. And though I bestow all my goods to feed the poor, and though I give my body to be burned, a .d have not charity, it profiteth me nothing. Charity suffereth long an' is kind ; charity envieth not ; charity vaunteth not itself, is not puffed up, doth not behave itself unseemly, seeketh not her own, is not easily provoked, thinketh no evil, rejoiceth not in iniquity, but rejoiceth in the truth ; beareth all things, believeth all things, hopeth all things, endureth all things. Charity never faileth ; but whether there be prophecies, they shall fail ; whether there be tongues they shall cease ; whether there be knowledge, it shall vanish away. For we know in part, and we prophesy in part. But when that which is perfect is come, then that which is in part shall be done away. When I was a child, I spake as a child, I understood as a child, I thought as a child ; but when I became a man, I put away childish things. For now we see through a glass darkly ; but then, face to face. Now, I know in part ; but then shall I know even as also I am known. And now abideth faith, hope, charity, these three, but the greatest of these is charity.

POPE TO ATTERBURY.

POPE TO ATTERBURY.

Once more I write to you, as I promised, and this once, I fear, will be the last. The curtain will soon be drawn between my friend and me, and nothing left but to wish you a long good night. May you enjoy a state of repose in this life not unlike that sleep of the soul which some have believed is to succeed it, where we lie utterly forgetful of that world from which we are gone, and ripening for that to which we are to go. If you retain any memory of the past, let it only image to you what has pleased you best; sometimes present a dream of an absent friend, or bring you back an agreeable conversation. But, upon the whole, I hope you will think less of the time past than of the future, as the former has been less kind to you than the latter infallibly will be. Do not envy the world your studies; they will tend to the benefit of men against whom you can have no complaint—I mean of all posterity, and perhaps, at your time of life, nothing else is worth your care. What is every year of a wise man's life but a censure or critic upon the past? Those whose date is shortest live long enough to laugh at one half of it. The boy despises the infant, the man the boy, the philosopher both, and the Christian all. You may now begin to think your manhood was too much of a puerility, and you will never suffer your age to be but a second infancy. The toys and bubbles of your childhood are hardly now more below you than those toys of our riper and of our declining years—the drums and rattles of ambition and the dirt and bubbles of avarice. At this time, when you are cut off from a little society, and merely a citizen of the world at large, you should bend your talents not to serve a party, or a few, but all mankind. Your genius should mount above that mist in which its participation and neighbourhood with earth long involved it. To shine abroad and to heaven, ought to be the business and the glory of your present situation. Remember it was at such a time that the greatest lights of antiquity dazzled and blazed the most, in their retreat, in their exile, or in their death. But, why do I talk of dazzling or blazing? It was then that they did good, that they gave light, and that they became guides to mankind. These aims alone are worthy of spirits truly great; and such, I therefore hope, will be yours. Resentment, indeed, may remain, perhaps cannot be quite extinguished, even in the noblest minds. But revenge never will harbour there; higher principles than those of the first, and better principles than those of the latter, will infallibly influence men whose thoughts and whose hearts are enlarged, and cause them to prefer the whole to any part of mankind, especially to so small a part as one's single self. Believe me, my lord, I look upon you as a spirit entered into another life—as one just upon the edge of immortality, where the passions and affections must be much more exalted, and where you ought to despise all little views, and all mean retrospects. Nothing is worth your looking back; and, therefore, look forward, and make, as you can, the world look after you, but take care that it be not with pity, but with esteem and admiration.

Address by Sir WILLIAM ARMSTRONG, C.B.

modus
vivendi

ADDRESS by Sir William Armstrong, C.B., *on*
" Social Matters, Past, Present, and Future," delivered
at the Annual Conference of the Northern Union of
Mechanics' Institutes, Elswick, Newcastle-upon-Tyne,
August 1883.

Gentlemen—

In the address delivered to you at Alnwick by Lord Percy in 1878 he remarked that men are always more sensible of the ills they labour under than of the blessings they enjoy. This is true in all the affairs of life. However much we mitigate the ills we suffer, our discontent at what remains continues unabated. I do not mean to say that discontent with our surroundings is without its use, seeing that it spurs us on to improve our condition ; but we do not in general recognise our progress, and we therefore scarcely do ourselves justice. Material progress is more palpable than moral progress, and therefore less liable to be ignored ; but history shows that, while this country has been advancing in science and the useful arts, and thereby enabling itself to maintain a population enormously increased in number and yet better fed, better clothed, and better housed than at any former period, it has also been improving almost as rapidly in its social and moral condition. To go no further back than the early part of the last century, we find that the state of morality and the habits of the people of this country were incomparably worse than at present. At that period bull-baiting, boar-baiting, cock-fighting, and cock-throwing, were the favourite sports of the people. The gentry were ignorant, coarse-mannered, and dissipated. Profligacy and a false sense of honour, leading to frequent duels, were distinctive of men of fashion. Housebreakers and highwaymen—the Jack Sheppards and Dick Turpins of the day—were popular heroes. Street outrages were of constant occurrence, with the lower classes for plunder, and with the higher for amusement founded on drunken revelry. The criminal laws were of the most sanguinary description, there being no less than 160 offences punishable with death. Executions, therefore, were fearfully numerous, and the depraved taste of the day rendered them enjoyable spectacles to all classes of the people. Those dens of villainy called sanctuaries, in which criminals could take refuge from justice, were not yet wholly abolished. Debtors were imprisoned until they could satisfy their creditors to the uttermost farthing, and were subject to the most scandalous extortions and oppressions on the part of their jailers. The sanitary state of the prisons, both for debtors and felons, was so bad as to give rise to frequent outbreaks of jail-fever, which often spread with destructive effect far beyond the prison walls. The severities practised in the Army and the Navy were shocking, and kidnapping for the latter was a usual practice. The slave-trade was not only sanctioned by public opinion, but was protected and encouraged by Acts of Parliament, and it is computed that 70,000 negroes were yearly torn from their homes and sold into slavery by English traders. In and out of Parliament jobbery and corruption were universal. Charitable institutions were rare, and the sufferings of the poor were treated by the ruling classes with indifference. The penal and disabling laws against Catholics and Dissenters were atrocious. Perpetual imprisonment on the evidence of a paid informer was the penalty on a Catholic priest discharging the functions of his office. In Ireland the oppression of the Catholics was carried to such an extreme that they were deprived of all political rights, were excluded from nearly all professions, and were denied the right of educating their children in their own faith. Their prelates were banished and forbidden to return under pain of death in the horrible form affixed to high treason. In Scotland religious fanaticism reigned supreme amongst the various sects calling themselves Christian, and gave rise to alternate persecutions, always shamefully violent and vindictive.

If we turn from this picture and contemplate the state of things at the present day, we see what a contrast is presented in our favour. Surely we may indulge ourselves by taking stock of our present moral condition, and appreciating the enormous gains we have made during this brief historical period. Nor has this moral amelioration been confined to our own country or to the period I have surveyed. All Europe has been improving, and if we carry our retrospect still further back we quickly come to the time when multitudes of wretched old women were burnt for witchcraft—when insane people were treated as demoniacs or beings outside the pale of humanity—when prisoners who refused to plead were slowly pressed to death by increasing weights upon their bodies—when confessions of guilt were wrung from innocent people by torture, and when the same means were used to extort false accusations—when religious persecutions assumed the dimensions of national devastations—when wars were waged for mere spoliation, and when mercy to the vanquished was the exception and not the rule. Still going back in time, we pass through the feudal period, characterised by grinding oppression and savage laws, when nearly every occupation but that of arms was deemed ignoble, and when wager of battle and ordeal of fire were the approved methods of deciding questions of right and justice. Then our retrospect carries us through the dark ages of history, when the light of civilisation became almost extinct, and was only kept alive by the institutions of the Catholic Church, to which our grateful acknowledgment is due for the part it acted at that period. Next we come to the horrible time of the later Roman Empire, distinguished by its unbridled sensuality and its hideous cruelty—when Roman patricians, and even Roman ladies, as well as the Roman populace, gloated over the bloody fights of gladiators in the amphitheatres, and with up-turned thumbs decreed the slaughter of every vanquished combatant who failed to minister sufficiently to their cruel pleasure. Still worse, when human beings (often martyrs to religion) were worried to death by wild beasts or subjected to every variety of torment at the public games for the entertainment of the people. If we continue to travel back in time beyond this hideous period, we come to the better epoch of the Roman Commonwealth, when civic virtues and a strong sense of duty were in the ascendant; but in the stoic virtue of that age there was no place for those emotional virtues which Christianity inculcates, and which are so highly esteemed at the present day. In ancient Greece, also, there was a better state of things than prevailed at a later date. We have there the spectacle of a people unsurpassed either before or since in the practice of the fine arts, and in the cultivation of metaphysical philosophy ; but science and the useful arts still lay dormant, and we find little in the moral character of the Greeks to excite our sympathy or admiration. A few steps further back and history fades away into barbarism.

From all this we may perceive that, although fluctuations may occur, the natural course of human affairs is one of amelioration, and that we are not justified in affixing the stigma of pessimism to the order of nature in its relation to humanity, as some modern writers are inclined to do.

And now let us return from the contemplation of the past to that of the present. One thing which distinguishes the age in which we live is its spirit of toleration. There is probably no one cause which has been so fruitful of suffering and injustice as the constant attempts which have been made for 1500 years to coerce belief on religious subjects. In Roman Catholic countries, where infallible authority is acknowledged in matters of faith, persecution may have some show of a logical basis ; but in Protestant countries, where the right of private judgment on spiritual subjects in conceded, prosecution for alleged error of belief is as irrational as it is wicked. Happily, prosecution, even in Catholic countries, has now almost entirely died out ; but denunciation, which is closely akin to it, still remains, even in our own enlightened National Church. But even in this case it is only as a relic of antiquity that the formulary which is chiefly chargeable with the offence finds a place in the beautiful Liturgy of the English Church. Christianity has grown more Christian since the Athanasian Creed was composed. Compare its damnatory clauses with the well-known words of a modern poet :—

> " Let not this weak, unknowing hand
> Presume Thy bolts to throw,
> And deal damnation round the land
> On each I judge Thy foe,"

then say which are most in accordance with the Christian spirit.

Another prominent feature in the morality of this day is the repugnance to cruelty of every kind, whether inflicted on men or animals. In the last century vivisection was practised in the most reckless and unnecessary manner, and scarcely a protest was raised against it. Now its practice, although mercifully performed under anæsthetics, is regulated by legislation, and there is danger of the restrictions upon it being carried to such an unreasoning length as to make the mitigated sufferings of animals of greater consideration than the advancement of medical and surgical knowledge, by which alone the diseases of humanity can be counteracted or alleviated. So also with regard to corporal punishment, which in the last century was inflicted in the most pitiless manner, both in the Army and Navy as well as on civilian offenders. Now it is abolished in both services, and even the whipping of a schoolboy or the moderate flogging of a hardened criminal is apt to meet with unmerite censure. Nothing can more strongly indicate the growth of the emotioua virtues than this aversion to cruelty ; but it must be confessed that there is danger of its being carried too far, and degenerating into a weak sentiment-ality, unsuited to the rough world in which it is our destiny to live.

But the thing which pre-eminently does honour to the present century is the great educatioual movement which has originated within very recent years, and is still undergoing development. It is not only that school education is provided for and enforced, but Mechanics' Institutes and Free Libraries have *every*where arisen to afford the means of following up the elementary education received at school. Sufficient time has not yet elapsed to enable us to judge of the effects of the movement. That it will do much good is unquestionable, but that the good will be unmixed with harm is by no means certain. There is an inveterate tendency in public opiniou to push a good thing too far, and I think there is danger of men being over-educated for the humbler positions which must be filled by great numbers of the popula-tion. That elementary education ought to be universal may be freely ad-mitted, but it is of far more importance that children should be thoroughly grouuded in rudiments than that they should be pushed beyond them. Those who possess exceptional powers will always be enabled, by the facilities now *every*where afforded, to practice self-education in after-life to any extent that may be required to satisfy their aspirations : but to attempt too high a standard at school will not only tend to produce a distaste for menial offices, but will involve keeping the pupils at school beyond the time at which the business of life should be commenced. This, I think, is to be deprecated, and that, as a rule, school education for the mass of the people should not be pro-longed beyond the limit prescribed by tenderuess of age, and consequent unfitness for labour.

I am unwilling to touch upon the question of religious education, but I cannot avoid doing so without appearing to ignore its importance. In the vast majority of cases religious belief is determined by parentage—and it is very right that it should be so, seeing that it is impossible for a child to renounce the religion of the family without doing violence to those ties of the early home which generally exercise so favourable an influence on the moral character through life. If the parents be sufficiently rich to pay for the edu-cation of their children, they have the option of sending them to denomina-tional schools where their own tenets are recognised : but when they cannot afford the necessary expense, and the State steps in and insists upon the child being educated at the public expense, the difficulty arises as to what the religious part of the instruction shall be, for it is impossible to provide for every variety of religious opinion held by the parents. A great deal of rancorous controversy has been raised upon this question, which is obviously one which can only be met by compromise ; and as we hear so much less of the difficulty now than formerly, we may conclude that by mutual concession a *modus vivendi* has been arrived at.

In connection with the religious aspect of education the important question also arises as to whether it will increase or diminish diversity of belief and general scepticism. There can be no doubt that education, by bringing the reflective faculties into play, disposes men to be critical in their beliefs. In these days of almost universal toleration the fullest freedom of discussion is permitted upon the most sacred questions so long as it is conducted in a spirit consonant with the solemnity of the subject. The literature which deals with such topics is greatly on the increase, and will continue to increase with the growing demand which extended education will create. Both sides of every debateable point will be presented, and men will more and more exercise their reason upon matters concerning which they have hitherto been chiefly guided by authority. What the effect of this untrammelled criticism may be I will not venture to predict; but of this we may rest assured, that the religious element in the human mind will not be uprooted. The star-filled heavens and a sense of man's responsibility were things which filled the philosophic mind of Kant with awe. The thoughts which they inspire will always lead men out of the narrow sphere of their own experiences into the boundless region of mystery which surrounds them, while the fear of the future will ever be associated with wrong-doing. Nor does it seem possible that mankind will ever accept as their creed that all the beauties, the harmonies, and the adaptations of Nature, down to the very constitution of matter, are the outgrowth of blind causation, or that the innumerable coincidences necessary to the existence of a complex and orderly universe can be rationally explained on the fortuitous basis of eternal duration. Still less are they ever likely to concur in believing that the supremacy of the human mind over matter, its profound speculations and its imaginative creations, together with its passionate emotions and aspirations, are all reducible (both as cause and effect) to mere atomic motion, and that Chemistry and Mechanics lie at the root of all things. Until such creeds gain the ascendency, men will reason from their own minds to an infinite mind, and religion will continue to exercise an elevating influence on our race.

To speak generally on the question of human progress, there seems to be no reason for taking a desponding view. The world will never be a paradise —least so in densely populated countries; but we may take comfort in thinking that misery emanating from our own vices is on the decrease. At the present moment the greatest evil that we in this country labour under is that of intemperance, to which it is not too much to say that half the crime, poverty, and misery of the country is attributable. The waste of national resources which it involves is as great as its demoralising effect. According to the average of recent years, the annual sum spent upon alcoholic liquors is about 130 millions sterling, which appears to be about as much as the cost of all the beef and the bread we consume in a year. If we concede everything that can be said in favour of alcohol used in moderation, it would be impossible to justify our spending upon a stimulant even one-fourth as much as we spend upon the two chief articles of our food. But, to be liberal, let us say that forty millions a-year might be beneficially appropriated to the supply of alcoholic liquors. Even under that admission we have to deplore a waste of ninety millions a-year, the chief part of which is sacrificed to the demon of drunkenness. We have also to take into account the cost of the crime, pauperism, idleness, and impaired powers of work, which follow in the train of intemperance. Although the amounts chargeable under these and other heads may be somewhat indefinite, they are not the less real, and statisticians place them at an appalling figure. In short, taking everything into consideration, the burden of drink, in a mere financial sense, probably weighs twice as heavily upon the nation as its Imperial taxation. It is gratifying, however, to observe that the tide does at length appear to have turned in favour of temperance. Amongst the wealthier classes Fashion has raised its potent voice against inebriation, and with other co-operating causes has almost banished it from that section of society; but amongst the poorer classes it is unfortunately still commonly regarded as excusable, or even as commendable, when associated with good fellowship. But under the refining influence of education and the strenuous efforts at suppression which are now being so laudably made by all our religious communities we may look for the establishment of a better atmosphere of opinion in the class which is now chiefly chargeable with intemperance, and when that takes place drunkenness will meet with surrounding discouragement, and repulsion will prove its irresistible foe.

Having thus endeavoured to place before you some of the salient features of past and present morality, I might extend my remarks at equal length to the region of the future, in which there is room for endless speculation; but under this head I shall confine myself to pointing out certain rocks ahead in the shape of unsolved problems, the issue of which it is extremely difficult to foresee. The rapid growth of our population is adverse to moral development, and, by increasing the competition for existence, it tends to the increase of poverty. The population of this country has more than doubled itself in the last fifty years, and, according to the best estimate that can be formed, it will be doubled again in the next seventy or eighty years. We are already overcrowded at the great centres of population, and the maintenance of the people is so completely beyond the productive capacity of the land, that nearly half the food we consume has to be imported from abroad. It is alarming to think what would become of us if the commerce upon which we are so entirely dependent should from any cause be interrupted; but if our position be critical now, with our thirty-five millions of inhabitants, what will it be in the middle of the next century, when we may anticipate a population twice as great as the present? Even then we shall be going on increasing in numbers, unless previously overtaken by disaster, and a crisis must apparently come, when further multiplication must be controlled by legislation, whatever violation of liberty and sentiment may be involved. In a state of nature, famine and pestilence keep down excessive increase, but we use all our ingenuity and our energies to banish those visitations without supplying any milder substitute. It is customary to speak of emigration as the remedy, but emigration is already in full operation, and does extremely little in reducing the increase. Moreover, the people of the countries available for emigration are multiplying almost as fast as we are, and in some cases even faster, so that the vacant places of the earth available for man's habitation are being rapidly filled. If, therefore, the growth of population be not arrested, the time must come when emigration on a large scale must cease for want of places to go to, unless, indeed, we resort to the old expedient of force, and fight for possession of available ground; but this would be incompatible with the continued progress of morality.

There is also another population difficulty which demands consideration. In a highly civilised and compassionate state of society there is a benevolent tendency to bolster up the weak and infirm, or in other words, to save the inferior members of our race from the extinction which nature would decree. By so doing, we act in diametrical opposition to that policy of selection which, in the management of domesticated animals, works such amazing improvement in their qualities. A degeneracy of our species, either mental or physical, would be deplorable; but how to prevent it under the mild sway of philanthropy, or how to take advantage of the principle of selection for the further development of our powers, is beyond my ability to conjecture. We can only hope that time and the growth of knowledge will bring a solution of this and other social problems,